IN THE
MONTH
OF
KISLEV

IN THE MONTH OF KISLEV

A Story for Hanukkah

by

NINA JAFFE

illustrated by

LOUISE AUGUST

VIKING

Thank you to Professor David G. Roskies of the Jewish Theological Seminary,
who read this text for background authenticity. Special thanks to Susan
Melvoin, Saul Rosenberg, and my editor, Deborah Brodie.   —N.J.

The art was prepared as woodcuts painted in full-color oils on paper.

VIKING
Published by the Penguin Group
Penguin Books USA Inc.,
375 Hudson Street, New York, New York 10014, U.S.A.
Penguin Books Ltd, 27 Wrights Lane, London W8 5TZ, England
Penguin Books Australia Ltd, Ringwood, Victoria, Australia
Penguin Books Canada Ltd, 10 Alcorn Avenue, Toronto, Ontario, Canada M4V 3B2
Penguin Books (N.Z.) Ltd, 182–190 Wairau Road, Auckland 10, New Zealand

Penguin Books Ltd, Registered Offices: Harmondsworth, Middlesex, England

First published in 1992 by Viking Penguin, a division of Penguin Books USA Inc.

3   5   7   9   10   8   6   4   2

Text copyright © Nina Jaffe, 1992
Illustrations copyright © Louise August, 1992

Library of Congress Cataloging-in-Publication Data
Jaffe, Nina.   In the month of Kislev : a story for Hanukkah /
by Nina Jaffe; illustrated by Louise August.   p.   cm.
Summary: A rich, arrogant merchant takes the family of a poor
peddler to court and learns a lesson about the meaning of Hanukkah.
I S B N 0 - 6 7 0 - 8 2 8 6 3 - 7
[1. Hanukkah—Fiction.]   I. August, Louise, ill.
PZ7.J1534In 1992 [E]—dc20   91-45804 CIP AC

Printed in Hong Kong   Set in 14 point Cheltenham

To my parents—
Grace and Marc—
with love.
—N.J.

To Mom, Tanta, Peter,
Danny, Rani, and Roy—
with love.
—L.A.

Once in Poland there was a peddler named Mendel. He and his wife, Rivkah, and their three children—Leah, Gittel, and Devorah—lived in a small hut at the edge of their town. Mendel worked hard, traveling to villages near and far, selling the pots and pans, handkerchiefs, and trinkets that he carried in his great sack. Rivkah worked hard, too, to keep their children clothed and fed, but it wasn't easy, on the little they had.

In that same town, there lived a lumber merchant named Feivel. He too had three children. But Feivel's wife had two servants to clean the house, and he himself had a coachman who drove him from one town to the next to see his customers.

Feivel was never happy to give charity. If a beggar came to his door, he would always find some excuse not to give alms. "I'm in a hurry," he would say. "I have to leave on business. Come back another day."

But on any day, Feivel's answer would still be the same. It wasn't the right way, but it was his way.

Each winter, the winds of Kislev blew cold and icy through the town. When the holiday of Hanukkah came, people would hurry home through the frosty air to light candles and say the blessings. Children would laugh and play for hours at a time as the wooden top—the dreidel—spun round and round. Then, out of the kitchen would come delicious *latkes*, potato pancakes. The children would eat, then count their Hanukkah *gelt*—little copper coins—and back to the dreidel they would go!

But this year, in one house in the town, there were no potato latkes, and no sounds of children laughing. This was the house of Mendel the peddler. Things had gone so badly for him that week that Rivkah could not buy even a single potato.

On the first night of Hanukkah, Leah, Gittel, and Devorah were walking home from the synagogue behind their father. On their way, they passed by the house of Feivel the merchant. As they turned the corner, they found themselves right underneath the kitchen window, and what an aroma met their cold little noses! It was the smell of golden latkes, just out of the pan, floating out into the air.

"Oh!" they said, "let's smell the latkes." For the three hungry children, it was as if they had eaten a whole plateful! Then they hurried home.

Inside their frail little hut, Rivkah lit the first candle and recited the blessings over it. The wind whistled through the cracks in the wall and almost blew the candle out. But the children didn't mind the wind. They were remembering the rich smell of latkes at Feivel's window.

Since there were no coins in the house, they played dreidel using small pebbles. Then, after kissing their parents good night, Leah went to the left side of the bed, Gittel went to the right, and Devorah crept into the middle. They huddled under their blankets and went to sleep, smiling happily.

"Look, Rivkah!" said Mendel to his wife. "The children are hungry, but they go to sleep smiling. What could this mean?" Rivkah only shook her head, but she wondered, too.

And so it went. On each of the first seven nights of Hanukkah, the children made sure to find their way through the streets to Feivel's house. Then they would rush to the window and breathe in the aroma of the latkes again. And on each night, the children went to bed smiling.

Finally, Mendel and Rivkah said to each other, "It must be
a Hanukkah miracle," and spoke no more about it.

15

Now it happened that on the eighth night, as the children stood beneath the window, the cook of the house looked outside and saw their faces. "Master! Mistress! Come quickly! There are some beggar children smelling *our* latkes!"

16

When Feivel came to the window and saw the children, he began to shout angrily. "So! The three of you have been stealing the smell of my latkes! I won't have Mendel the peddler's children coming to my house and taking the smell of my food right out from under my nose! Why, it's like you're eating for nothing!"

And the very next day, Feivel and his wife and children
hauled Mendel and *his* wife and children to the house of the
rabbi. When the news got out, all the townspeople went there,
too, to see what would happen.

Rabbi Yonah was a kindly man, known throughout the town
for his wisdom and fair judgments. He sat at his wooden desk,
which was piled high with books and scrolls, and listened
calmly as Feivel presented his complaint.

"Rabbi," Feivel cried angrily, "these children have been smelling my latkes for the entire holiday! It's as if they took the food right out from under our noses."

"Well," said Rabbi Yonah, "and what do you want me to do about it?"

"Rabbi," said Feivel, "I don't mind if they take the smell, but at least they should pay for it. Yes, let them pay a fine."

"And how much do you propose this fine to be?" asked the
rabbi, ever so softly.

"What's right is right," said Feivel. "I demand fair payment.
Let them pay me one ruble for each time they stood under the
window. For the eight nights of Hanukkah, that would be eight
rubles!"

"Eight rubles," whispered the townspeople. "Feivel the merchant wants Mendel the peddler to pay eight rubles for the smell of his latkes!"

Mendel could hardly speak. "But, Rabbi," he said at last, "I do not have eight rubles to give. I barely have a kopek to my name as it is. How can I pay this fine?"

Rabbi Yonah tapped his fingers on the desk for a moment. Then he looked through the window at the crowd that had gathered outside his house. He opened the door and spoke to all the townspeople.

"Friends and neighbors," he said, "look in your pockets. Who has Hanukkah *gelt*?"

Everyone—mothers, fathers, grandparents, and children—reached into their coats or trousers. Even into their boots. One by one, they dropped their little copper coins into a small brown bag that the rabbi held out to them. After he had collected all the coins, he tied up the little bag with a string. And then Rabbi Yonah began to do a very strange thing.

He began to shake the bag. He shook the bag, and he shook the bag—one minute, two minutes, three minutes—until the coins jingled like a little music box.

The people looked at each other with wide eyes.

"Has our rabbi gone crazy?" they whispered. "What can he be doing?"

Finally, he stopped. Silence filled the room. The rabbi turned to Feivel and said, "There, my friend. What's right is right. You asked for fair payment and you have received it. We have paid for the smell of your Hanukkah latkes with the sound of Hanukkah *gelt*! Now go home, and try to do good in the world."

When he heard these words, Feivel turned around and walked slowly out the door, with his face to the ground. As the townspeople walked home, they nodded to each other, "How wise our rabbi is!"

After that day, any beggar who came to Feivel's house was given a good meal and a warm blanket to take home. The charity box in the synagogue was never empty, thanks to him.

And every year, when the winds of Kislev blew through the town, Feivel and his wife and children, and Mendel and his wife and children would light the menorah, play dreidel, and eat plates and plates of potato latkes.

Together.

About This Book

The word "Hanukkah" means dedication. The winter holiday of Hanukkah, which falls in the Hebrew month of Kislev (November or December) is a celebration of many things: light, warmth, religious freedom, and the right to be different, even unique. It celebrates a real historical event which took place more than 2100 years ago—a war of liberation in which a small Jewish army, led by the Maccabees, was able to defeat a huge Syrian-Greek army, led by a cruel general, Antiochus.

According to legend, the Jews returned to the Holy Temple in Jerusalem to clean and rebuild it. But when the priests went to light the menorah, the seven-branched lamp, they found only a small jar of oil, enough to last for one day, in all the city. While a messenger was sent to find more oil, the people and the priests rekindled their precious lamp. To the wonder of all, the oil in the lamp lasted a full eight days, giving enough time for the messenger to return.

This, then, is the event that came to be known as the miracle of Hanukkah. Every year, Jews all over the world remember and honor this event by lighting a menorah in homes and synagogues. Each night, one more candle is lit (a ninth candle—the *shammash* is used to help light all the others), until on the eighth night, a fully lighted menorah shines in the window, for all to see.

There are many lovely customs associated with the celebration of Hanukkah. Jewish communities have special foods, like the *latkes* of Eastern Europe, *loukomades* of Greece, and *sufganiyot* of Israel. All of these dishes are cooked in oil, to remind us of the miracle. In my house, as in many other Jewish homes, we play dreidel. This is a game of chance using a metal or wooden top and Hanukkah *gelt*, or money (sometimes chocolate candies or unshelled nuts are used). The letters on the top, *nun, gimmel, hay,* and *shin* stand for the Hebrew sentence, *"Nes gadol hayah sham,"* which means "a great miracle happened there." The letters also stand for how much you are going to win or lose when the dreidel stops spinning.

Traditionally, Hanukkah has also been a special time for storytelling and riddles, as no work is done while the candles are burning. In the darkness of winter, when the days are short, and the nights are long and dark, it is good to be together with family and friends, singing out the joyous Hanukkah melodies, by the light and warmth of the menorah flames.